P9-DGC-194

Winnie the Pooh and the Blustery Day
Winnie the Pooh and the Honey Tree
Winnie the Pooh and a Day for Eeyore
Winnie the Pooh and Tigger Too

Winnie
the Pooh
CD Storybook

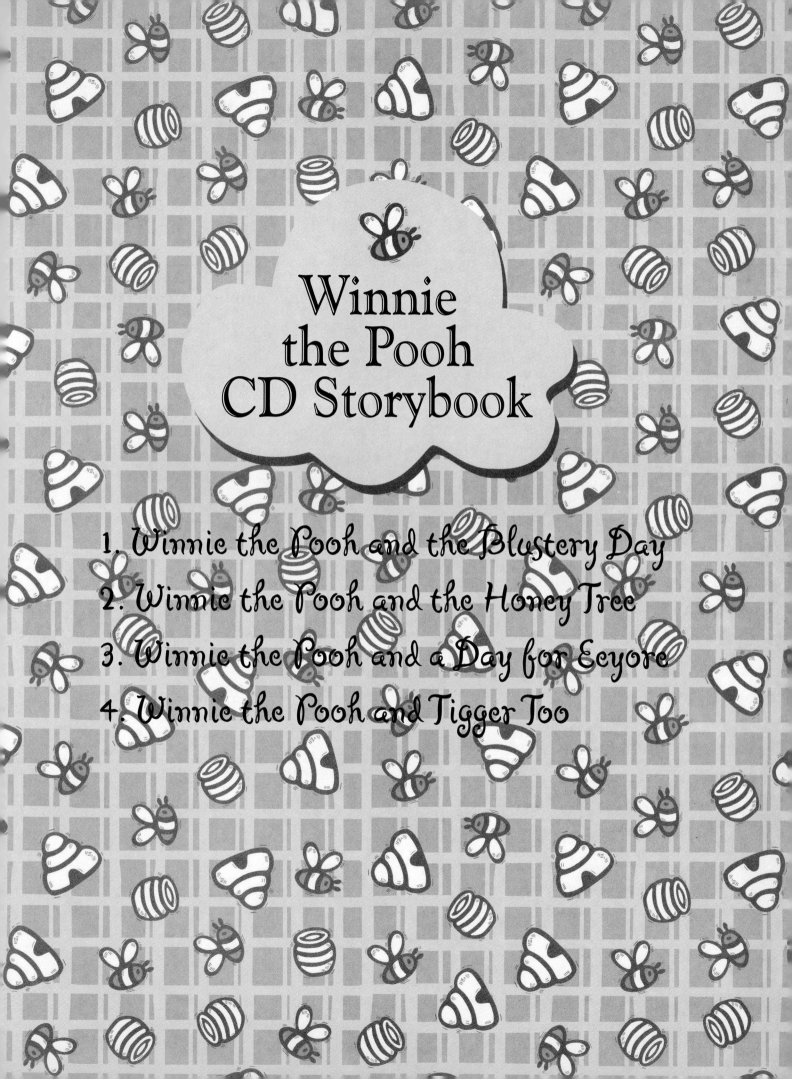

Winnie the Pooh CD Storybook

Disney.com

© Disney
Based on the 'Winnie the Pooh' works,
by A.A. Milne and E.H. Shepard.

Published 2001 by HINKLER BOOKS PTY LTD
17-23 Redwood Drive, Dingley, Victoria, 3172, Australia
ISBN: 1 86515 3036

All Rights Reserved. Without limiting the rights under copyright above,
no part of this publication may be reproduced, stored in or introduced
into a retrieval system, or transmitted in any form or by any means
(electronic, mechanical, photocopying, recording or otherwise), without
the prior written permission of the Walt Disney Company.
Printed and bound in China.

Contents

Golden Slumbers

Golden Slumbers, kiss your eyes,
Smiles await you when you rise.
Sleep little baby, don't you cry,
and I will sing a lullaby.

Rain, Rain, Go Away

Rain, rain, go away,
Come again another day;
Rain, rain, go away,
Little Piglet wants to play.

Winnie the Pooh and the Blustery Day

Winnie the Pooh, or "Pooh" for short, lived with his friends
in the Hundred Acre Wood. One very blustery day, when
the winds decided to stir things up, Pooh went to visit his
thinking spot.

As Pooh sat there, trying hard to think of something, up popped his friend, Gopher. "Say, Pooh, if I were you, I'd think about skedaddlin' out of here. It's Windsday, see?"

Pooh thought that sounded like a lot of fun.
"Then I think I shall wish everyone a happy Windsday.
And I will begin with my dear friend, Piglet."

The wind was blowing very hard as Pooh neared
Piglet's house. "Happy Windsday, Piglet. I see you're
sweeping leaves."
"Yes, Pooh. But it's hard. This is a very unfriendly wind."

Just then, a big gust blew Piglet up into the air. Pooh
watched in surprise. "Where are you going, Piglet?"
"I don't know, Pooh. Oh, dear!" Pooh tried to help, but
when he grabbed Piglet's sweater, it began to unravel!

Piglet flew like a kite over the countryside, with Pooh
dragging behind. "Oh Piglet!" The two went right through
Eeyore's house and Rabbit's carrot patch.

Then with the blusteriest, gustiest gust of all, Piglet and Pooh were blown right up to Owl's house in a tall tree.

"Pooh! Piglet! This is a special treat! I so rarely get
visitors up here. Do come in." Owl opened his window
and in blew Pooh and Piglet.

The wind blew harder and harder until finally Owl's tree, along with his house, crashed to the ground. Everyone from the Hundred Acre Wood came to help Owl, but only gloomy old Eeyore seemed to know what to do.

"If you ask me, and nobody has, I say when a house looks
like that, it's time to find another one. A thankless job,
but I'll find a new one for him." And off he plodded.

Finally the blustery day turned into a blustery night. To Pooh, it was an uncomfortable night full of uncomfortable noises. And one of the noises was a sound he had never heard before. "Gr-r-r-rowl!"

Pooh got up and went to his door to investigate.
"Hello, out there! Oh, I hope nobody answers."

Just then a funny-looking animal bounced into the room.
"Hi, I'm Tigger. T-I-double Guh-ER."

Pooh put down his pop-gun. "You scared me."
"Sure I did! Everyone's scared of Tiggers!"
"Well, what's a Tigger?"
"Glad you brought that up, chum!" Then Tigger bounced
around the room to show Pooh what a Tigger was.

Tigger stopped bouncing. "Did I say I was hungry?"
"Not for honey, I hope."

"Yuck! Tiggers don't like that icky, sticky stuff.
Well, I better be bouncing along.
T.T.F.N.! Ta-ta for now!"

The wind continued to blow. There was a clap of thunder and
it began to rain. And it rained, and it rained, and it rained.
By morning, the Hundred Acre Wood was flooded.

Pooh tried to rescue his honey by eating it all for breakfast. He was upside-down, licking the bottom of the last pot, when the water floated him right out his front door.

At Piglet's house, the water was coming in through the
window. He wrote a message and put it into a bottle.
The message read, *Help Piglet (Me)*. The bottle floated
out of his house and out of sight.

Christopher Robin lived high on a hill where the water couldn't reach. So that was where everyone from the Hundred Acre Wood gathered. Before long Christopher Robin discovered Piglet's bottle and read the message. "Owl, fly over to Piglet's house and tell him we'll plan a rescue."

As Owl flew over the flood, he spotted two tiny objects below. One was Piglet, standing on a chair, and the other was Pooh, still upside-down in his honey pot.

Owl called down to them and told them of the rescue.
"Be brave, little Piglet!"
"Thank you, Owl, but it's awfully hard to be brave
when you're such a small animal."

Pooh and Piglet eventually floated to the very spot where
Christopher Robin was waiting. "Pooh, you rescued Piglet! That
was a very brave thing to do. You're a hero!"
"I am?"
"Yes. And so I shall give you a hero party!"

Just as the hero party began, Eeyore arrived with news.
"I found a house for Owl. If you want to follow me,
I'll show it to you."

Eeyore led them through the woods and, to everyone's surprise,
stopped in front of Piglet's house.
"This is it."
Pooh tried to convince Piglet to speak up.
"No, Pooh. This house belongs to our good friend, Owl.
I shall live…shall live…"

"You shall live with me." Pooh put his arm around his little friend. Christopher Robin was especially proud. "That was a very grand thing to do, Piglet - giving your house to Owl."

And so, the one-hero party became a two-hero party. Pooh was a hero for saving Piglet's life and Piglet was a hero for giving Owl his grand home in the beech tree.

Hip hip hooray! For the Piglet! And the Pooh!

Round and Round the Garden

Round and round the garden
Like a teddy bear;
One step, two step,
Tickle you under there!

Pooh and Friends Come Out to Play

Pooh and friends come out to play;
The moon does shine as bright as day.
Leave your supper and leave your sleep;
And join your friends who jump and leap!
Come with a whoop and come with a call;
Come with goodwill or not at all.
Up the ladder and down the tree;
Let's all eat honey loaf for our tea.
You find the milk and I'll find the flour;
And we'll have a pudding in half an hour!

Winnie the Pooh and the Honey Tree

Winnie the Pooh lived in an enchanted forest under the name of Sanders, which means he had the name over the door and he lived under it. Now when Pooh heard his Pooh Coo Clock, he knew it was time for something.

"Think, think, think. Oh, yes. Time for my stoutness exercise."

Pooh stood in front of his mirror and tried to touch his toes.
"Up, down and touch the ground. Up, down and touch the ground..."
But instead of making him thin, the exercise made Pooh hungry.
So he went to his cupboard, got down a honey jar, and inspected his
honey supply. "Oh, bother. Empty again. Only the sticky part's left."

Pooh put his head in the jar and tried to get at the last bit of honey, when he heard a buzzing sound.
"That buzzing noise means something. And the only reason for making a buzzing noise that I know of is because you're a ...a bee! And the only reason for being a bee is to make honey."

Pooh followed the bee outside to a nearby tree.
High in a hole near the top, sat a beehive full of honey.
"And the only reason for making honey is so I can eat it."
So Pooh began to climb the honey tree.

He climbed and he climbed. And just as Pooh neared
the beehive, the branch he was standing on broke,
and down went Pooh, into a very prickly bush below.
"Oh, bother."
Pooh brushed the prickles from his nose and decided to
go ask Christopher Robin for help.

"Christopher Robin, I was wondering if you had such a
thing as a balloon about you."
Christopher Robin happened to have just the thing.
"But what do you want a balloon for?"
"Honey. I shall fly like a bee, up to the honey tree."

Pooh ran off to a very muddy place near the honey tree, and
Christopher Robin followed. Pooh rolled around and around until
he was covered with mud from his nose to his toes. Christopher
Robin scratched his head and wondered what Pooh was up to.
"What are you supposed to be, Pooh?"
"A little black rain cloud, of course. Now, would you aim
me at the bees, please?" Christopher Robin handed Pooh
the balloon and launched him into the air.

Pooh rose higher and higher toward the hole in the top of the honey tree. And while he hovered outside, a bee flew from the hive and landed on Pooh's nose.

"Christopher Robin, I think the bees suspect something. Maybe it would help with the deception if you would open your umbrella and say, 'Tut, tut, it looks like rain.' "

So Christopher Robin opened his umbrella and paced back
and forth beneath it. "Tut, tut, it looks like rain!"
The little bee, however, was not fooled. He knew the difference
between a rain cloud and a hungry Pooh Bear. So, he flew at
Pooh and stung him directly on his softest spot.
"Oh!" Pooh swung left, then right, then quite by accident
swung his very sore bottom into the hole in the tree.
"Oh, dear. I'm stuck."

In no time, the bees inside the tree created a mighty force and they pushed Pooh out of the hole, sending him shooting across the sky. The balloon sputtered and Pooh came tumbling downward. "Oh, bother. I think I shall come down now."

Pooh fell from the sky with the bees in hot pursuit. Christopher
Robin gently caught him, and together they ran to the muddy place
and jumped in. Christopher Robin opened his umbrella and they hid
beneath it as the bees buzzed past. The bees did not bother them
any more that day.

Once Pooh began thinking about honey,
he just couldn't stop.
So, he made his way to Rabbit's house for a
light honey snack.

"Hello, Rabbit!"
"Oh, dear. Hello, Pooh Bear. What a surprise.
Well, how about lunch?"
Pooh sat himself down at the table and tied a napkin around his
neck. Rabbit knew perfectly well what Pooh was hungry for.

He reluctantly pulled out a honey jar and offered it to Pooh.
"Thank you, Rabbit. Just a small helping, please."
Pooh helped himself to Rabbit's honey, and he ate and he
ate and he ate and he ate, until there was no honey left.
"Not at all?" Not a drop.

Finally, in a very sticky voice, he excused himself.
"I must be going now. Good-bye, Rabbit."
Pooh thanked Rabbit and he turned to leave. But Pooh's
tummy, full of honey, only got halfway out of Rabbit's small
front door. "Oh, bother. I'm stuck."

Rabbit pushed at Pooh's round bottom, but it was no use.
"Oh, dear. Oh, dear. There's only one thing to do. I'll get
Christopher Robin." Rabbit hurried out of the side door to
find his friend.

In a short time, Rabbit returned with Christopher Robin.
"Cheer up, Pooh Bear. We'll get you out."
Christopher Robin took hold of Pooh, and Rabbit took hold
of Christopher Robin. And on the count of three-
One! Two! Three!- they pulled as hard as they could.
But Pooh wouldn't budge. "It's no use. I'm stuck."
Christopher Robin shook his head. "Pooh Bear, there's
only one thing to do - wait for you to get thin again."

Nobody knew how long it would take Pooh to get thin, so poor
Rabbit tried to make the best of the situation by decorating
Pooh's bottom with a picture frame and some antlers.
"There. A hunting trophy. Ahh...I know what it needs."
Rabbit then painted a face on Pooh's bottom.
It tickled, and Pooh wriggled. "Oh, Pooh. You messed
up my moose."

And while Rabbit got along with Pooh's back end, his front
end was visited by many friends, including Kanga and little Roo.
"Pooh, Roo has a little surprise for you." Roo handed Pooh a big
bouquet of flowers. Pooh took a deep sniff.
"Honey-suckle. Thank you, Roo."

Day after day, night after lonely night, Pooh waited to get thin.
And while he waited, who should pop up one night but his good
friend Gopher. "I'm working the swing shift, sonny. But now it's
time for my midnight snack."
Gopher opened his lunch box and inspected its contents, while
Pooh looked on with a hungry "feed me" sort of look. "Let's see
here…summer squash, succotash, spiced custard…and honey."

Pooh brightened at the sound of his favourite word.
"Honey? Could you spare a small smackeral?"
But before Pooh could attempt a taste, Rabbit whipped out
of his side door and planted a large sign next to Pooh.
"Don't feed the bear!"
Poor Pooh. Gopher quickly went back to work, and Pooh
continued his long, and very hungry, wait.

And then, one morning when Rabbit was beginning to think that he might never be able to use his front door again, it happenend. He leaned up against Pooh's bottom and...

"He budged! Christopher Crabin! Eh, ah, Chrostofer Raban!
He bidged! He badged! He boodged! Today is the day!"
Almost everyone in the Hundred Acre Wood came
running to help.

From inside his house, Rabbit pushed frantically on his end of
Pooh, while outside everyone else pulled on the other end.
"Heave-ho! Heave-ho!" They tugged and they pushed and they
pulled and they shoved with all their might, until suddenly...

Pooh shot out of the hole and flew high overhead into the treetops, where he landed in the hole in the honey tree.
Christopher Robin called from down below. "Don't worry, Pooh. We'll get you out."
"No hurry. Take your time!"

For you see, Pooh had landed right in the middle of the beehive and some very yummy honey.

"Yum, yum. Bears love honey, and I'm a Pooh Bear. Yum, yum, yum, yum. Time for something sweet."

Christopher Robin shook his head and grinned. "Silly old bear."

One, Two, Winnie the Pooh

One, two, Winnie the Pooh,
Three, four, shut the door,
Five, six, pick up sticks,
Seven, eight, lay them straight.

Nine, ten, remember when?
Eleven, twelve, dig and delve,
Thirteen, fourteen, Roo's cavorting,
Fifteen, sixteen, someone's missing.

Seventeen, eighteen, Kanga's waiting,
Nineteen, twenty, my tummy's empty!

Three Happy Friends

Three happy friends,
They sailed in an umbrella,
And if the umbrella had been stronger,
This poem would have been longer!

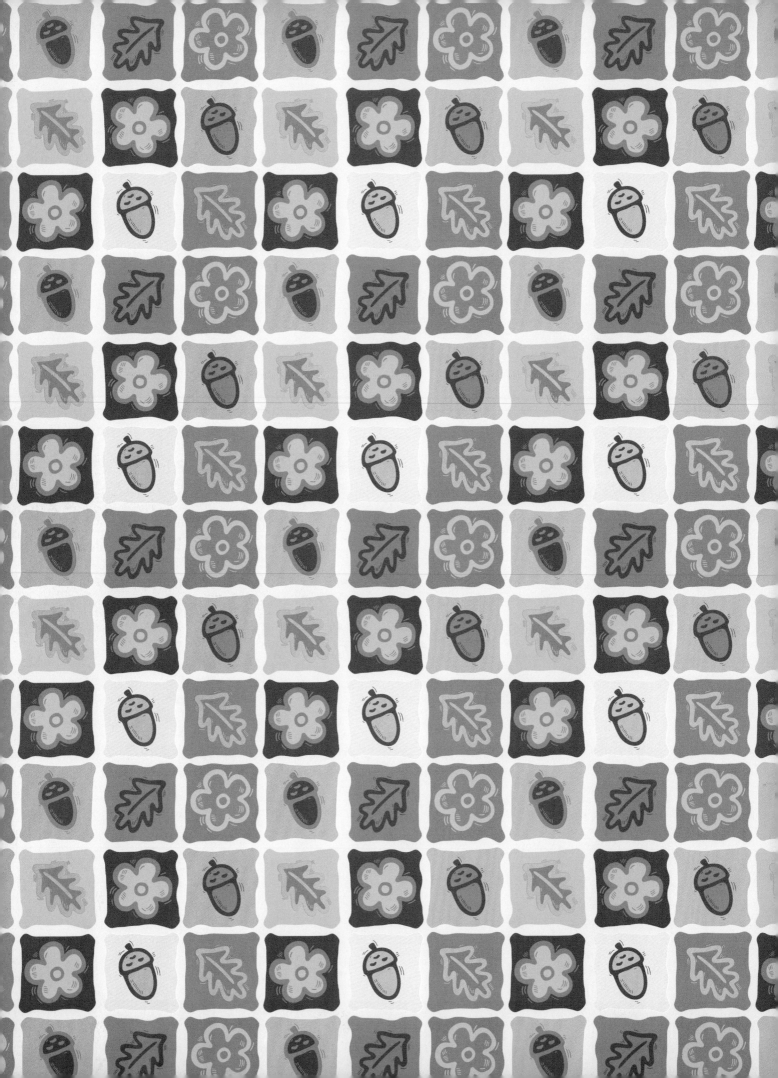

Winnie the Pooh
and a Day for Eeyore

One day, as Winnie the Pooh stood on the old wooden bridge that crossed the river that ran through the Hundred Acre Wood, he dropped a fir cone into the water.
Pooh watched it disappear then reappear on the other side of the bridge. "Now if I drop two cones, I wonder which will come out first."

Well, as Pooh quite expected, the big one came out
first and the little one came out last.
And that was how Pooh invented the game called
"Pooh Sticks," even though he began with fir cones.

Not long after that, Pooh and Piglet, Rabbit and Roo were
all playing Pooh Sticks together. Rabbit recited the rules.
"All right now. The first stick to pass all the way under the
bridge wins. On your marks ... get set ... go!"
Pooh anxiously waited to see which stick would come out first.
"I see your stick, Piglet! It's the grey one!"

But Pooh soon discovered that it wasn't a grey stick at all.
It was Eeyore's tail. And if you find Eeyore's tail, you can
be most assured of finding ... "Eeyore!"
"Don't pay any attention to me. Nobody ever does."

Now the problem was how to get Eeyore out of the water.
Pooh offered a suggestion. "If we all threw stones and things
into the river on one side of Eeyore, the stones would make
waves and the waves would wash him to the other side."
It was a most brilliant solution. "Thank you." You're welcome.
And the others quite agreed.

Pooh found a nice big boulder and rolled it onto the bridge.
Rabbit, as usual, gave the instructions.
"All right, Pooh, when I say 'now', you can drop it.
One ... two ... NOW!"

Unfortunately, the boulder hit Eeyore in the softest spot of his tummy ... and ... he sank. Pooh shook his head as he watched his friend disappear.

"Oh, dear. Perhaps it wasn't such a very good idea."

But just then, Piglet caught sight of Eeyore climbing up onto the riverbank. "Look! There he is!"

Of course, they all wanted to know how Eeyore had fallen in.
Emptying the water from one ear, the old grey donkey explained.
"I was thinking by the side of the river, minding my own
business, when I received a loud bounce."
Before anyone could make a guess as to what that meant, a
very bouncy Tigger came bouncing down the path and
bowled over the unsuspecting Rabbit. "Hello, Rabbit!"

"Tigger, did you bounce Eeyore?"
"No, I didn't. Really. I, uh, I just had a cough, see?
And besides, bouncing is what Tiggers do best!"
Rabbit nodded grimly. "Ah-ha! So, you did bounce Eeyore, eh,
Tigger?" "Some people have no sense of humour." And with that,
Tigger turned and bounced off down the path.

A very soggy Eeyore watched Tigger leave.
"Why should Tigger care? Nobody else does."
And while his friends puzzled over his unusual behaviour,
Eeyore followed the river back to his gloomy spot.
Pooh ran after him.

"Eeyore, what's the matter? You seem so sad."
"Why should I be sad? It's my birthday. The happiest day of the year. Can't you see all the presents? The cake? The candles and the pink sugar frosting?" Of course there were no presents, or cake, or candles, or pink sugar frosting.
"But don't worry about me, Pooh. Go and enjoy yourself."

Pooh felt very bad for Eeyore, so he hurried home as fast as he could to tell the others. When he arrived at his house, who should he find there but ... "Piglet!"

"Hello, Pooh! I was trying to reach the knocker."

"Let me do it for you." Pooh lifted the knocker and rapped on the door.

"Piglet, I found out what's troubling poor Eeyore. It's his birthday and nobody has taken any notice of it."
Now you'll remember that Pooh is a bear of very little brain.
"Well, Piglet, whoever lives here certainly takes a long time answering his door." "But Pooh, isn't this your house?"
"Oh, so it is!" Pooh opened the door and they went inside.

"Piglet, I must get poor Eeyore a present of some sort." Pooh
went directly to his cabinet and got down a nice big jar of honey.
"This should do very well. What are you going to give him, Piglet?"
"Perhaps I could give Eeyore a balloon. I have one at home."
Piglet trotted off in one direction to his house, and in the other
direction went Pooh with his jar of honey towards Eeyore's
gloomy spot.

Pooh had only travelled a short distance when a little voice from deep inside his tummy spoke to him. "Now then, Pooh, time for a little something." So Pooh had a little something, and then he had a little more and a little more, until he had taken the last lick from the inside of the honey jar. "Oh, bother. This jar seems to be missing something. Perhaps Owl can help."

At Owl's house, Pooh explained all about Eeyore's birthday.
Owl nodded wisely. "What are you giving him, Pooh?"
"I'm giving him this useful pot to keep things in. And I was
wondering if you could write something on it.
My spelling is wobbly."

So Owl wrote on the pot:
"A Happy Birthday, With Love from Pooh."
Pooh thanked Owl and happily went on his way, while Owl
flew off to tell Christopher Robin about Eeyore's birthday.
As Owl flew overhead, Piglet waved from down below,
holding tight to the bright red balloon he was taking to Eeyore.

"Hello, Owl! Many happy returns of Eeyore's... Ooff!"
He ran straight into the trunk of a tree. Piglet and the balloon
bounded up and down, up and down, until the balloon burst.
"Oh, dear. What shall I - ? How shall I - ? Well, perhaps Eeyore
doesn't like balloons very much." Piglet sadly gathered up the
flattened balloon and continued on his way.

It wasn't long until Piglet found Eeyore sitting under a tree.
"Good afternoon, Eeyore."
"Good afternoon, Piglet. If it is a good afternoon, which I doubt."
Piglet handed Eeyore what was left of the balloon.
"I'm very sorry. But when I was running to bring it, I fell down."
Eeyore looked at the balloon and smiled. "A birthday balloon?
For me? And it's red. My favourite colour."

Just then, Pooh arrived. "I've brought you a little present, Eeyore.
It's a useful pot, for putting things in."
"Like a balloon?" Eeyore picked up the balloon in his mouth,
dropped it in the pot, then took it out again. Pooh was very pleased
with himself. "I'm glad I thought of giving you a useful pot to put
things in." Piglet grinned a big grin. "And I'm glad I thought of
giving you something to put in a useful pot."

Later that day, Christopher Robin gathered everyone together to celebrate Eeyore's birthday, and he brought along a cake covered with pink sugar frosting. Eeyore made a wish and blew out all the candles. "Hooray!" Then Christopher Robin cut the cake and passed it around so that everyone had a piece.

Just then, a great "Halloo" was heard over the celebration.
Rabbit knew it could mean only one thing.
Sure enough, Tigger came bouncing along and knocked Rabbit to
the ground. Christopher Robin giggled.
"Hello, Tigger. We're having a party."
"A party? Oh, boy! Tiggers love parties! And cake!"
Rabbit glared at Tigger. "You've got a lot of nerve showing up
here after what you did to Eeyore. I think Tigger should leave."
But Christopher Robin had a better idea.
"I think we all ought to play Pooh Sticks!"

So they gathered on the old wooden bridge and played the game for many contented hours. And Eeyore, who had never played it before, won more times than anybody else.

But poor Tigger won none at all.
"Grrr.... Tiggers don't like Pooh Sticks."
It was getting late and Rabbit decided that it was time for them
all to be going home. Owl agreed. "Yes, quite right.
Congratulations, Eeyore. It's been a delightful party."

As Tigger trudged sadly home, Eeyore caught up to him.
"Tigger, I'd be happy to tell you my secret for winning at Pooh Sticks."
"You would?"
"It's very easy. You just have to let your stick drop in a 'twitch' sort
of way." Tigger laughed and bounced along after Eeyore.
"Oh, yeah! I forgot to twitch! That was my problem!"

Then, just on the other side of the hill, where no one else could
see, Tigger bounced Eeyore, because that's what Tiggers do best.
And Eeyore, with memories of a wonderful birthday,
didn't seem to mind a bit.

Honeypot, Honeypot

Honeypot, honeypot sat on a wall,
Honeypot, honeypot had a great fall.
All of Pooh's bandages, all of Pooh's glue,
Just couldn't make that poor honeypot new!

Knitting, Knitting

Knitting, knitting, one, two, three,
I knit scarves for Roo and me.
I love honey and I love tea;
Knitting, knitting, one, two, three.

Winnie the Pooh
and Tigger Too

Winnie the Pooh lived in an enchanted place called the Hundred Acre Wood. One day, while he was thinking in his thoughtful spot, he was bounced by a springy character with stripes.

"Hello, Pooh. I'm Tigger! T-I-double Guh-ER!"

"I know. You've bounced me before."

Tigger liked to bounce, especially on unsuspecting friends.
Piglet was sweeping leaves when Tigger bounced him.

All the leaves went flying. "Hello, Piglet! That was only a little bounce, you know. I'm saving my best one for Rabbit."
And Tigger bounded over to Rabbit's house.

Rabbit was happily working in his vegetable garden
when Tigger called out a greeting. "Hello, Long Ears!"

"No. no, Tigger! Don't bounce…!" But Rabbit couldn't stop
Tigger from bouncing. Vegetables went flying in all directions.

A very discouraged Rabbit sat down on the ground.
"Tigger, just look at my beautiful garden."
"Yuck! Messy, isn't it?" Tigger frowned in disgust.
"Messy? It's ruined! Oh, why don't you ever stop bouncing?"
"Why? That's what Tiggers do best!"
And off Tigger bounced down the road.

Rabbit was so upset about his garden that he called a
meeting at his house, which Pooh and Piglet attended.
"Attention, everybody! Something has got to be done about
Tigger's bouncing. And I have a splendid idea."

"We'll take Tigger for a long explore in the woods and lose him.
And when we find him, he'll be a more grateful Tigger,
an 'Oh, how can I ever thank you for saving me' Tigger.
And it will take the bounces out of him.

It was agreed. The next morning, Pooh, Piglet and Rabbit
took Tigger for an early misty-morning walk in the woods.
Tigger bounced up ahead.

Then, when Tigger wasn't looking, Rabbit,
Pooh and Piglet hid in a hollow log.

It wasn't long before Tigger noticed he was alone. "Now where do you suppose old Long Ears went to? Hallooo! Where are you fellas? Gee, they must have gotten lost." And Tigger bounced off to find his friends.

When all seemed clear, Rabbit crept out of the log and called
the others to join him. "You see? My splendid plan is working!
Now we'll go and save Tigger."
But as they walked on, they kept coming back to the same
sand pit. Pooh, who is a bear of very little brain, had a thought.
"Maybe the sand pit is following us, Rabbit."

"Nonsense, Pooh. I know my way through the forest."
And Rabbit left to prove he could find his way home.
After Rabbit had been gone awhile, Pooh felt a rumbling in
his tummy. "I think my honey pots are calling to me. Come on,
Piglet. My tummy knows the way home."
Just then, who should appear but Tigger.
He happily bounced Pooh and Piglet.
"I thought you fellas were lost!"

It turned out that the only one who was lost was Rabbit!
All alone in the dense woods, he jumped at every noise.

Rabbit grew more and more frightened.
The thick mist was filled with strange shapes and sounds.
Suddenly he heard "Hallooo!" Before he knew it, Rabbit was
found, and bounced, by an old familiar friend.

"Tigger! But you're supposed to be lost!"
"Oh, Tiggers never get lost, Bunny Boy. Come on, let's go home."
Rabbit took hold of Tigger's tail, and Tigger bounced him all
the way home. This time, Rabbit didn't seem to mind a bit.

Before long, winter came and transformed the Hundred Acre
Wood into a playground of white fluffy snow. Roo was so
anxious to play with Tigger that his mother, Kanga, barely
had time to tie a scarf around his neck. "Have him home
by nap time, Tigger."

"Don't worry, Mrs.Kanga. I'll take care of the little nipper."
Then off they bounced, because that's what Tiggers and
Roos do best!

Soon they came upon a frozen pond where Rabbit was skating
gracefully on the ice. Roo watched in amazement.
"Can Tiggers skate as fancy as Mr. Rabbit?"
"Sure, Roo. Why, that's what Tiggers do best!"

But when Tigger ran onto the ice, he slipped and skidded right into Rabbit, and they all went crashing right through Rabbit's front door! Tigger groaned.
"Tiggers don't like ice skating."

Tigger and Roo
looked for
something else that
Tiggers do best. Roo had
an idea. I'll bet you could
climb trees, Tigger!"
"Tiggers don't climb trees.
They bounce 'em!"
So Tigger and Roo
bounced all
the way to the top of a
tall tree. Suddenly, Tigger
realised just how far
down the ground actually was.
"Whoaa! Tiggers don't
like to bounce trees!"

Roo, however, thought
this was great fun.
He swung back
and forth, holding onto
Tigger's tail. "Wheee-ee!"
"Stop, kid! S-T-O-P!
You're rocking the forest!"

While Tigger was up in the tree, Pooh and Piglet were down below, tracking footprints in the snow. Piglet asked Pooh what they were tracking. "I won't know until I catch up with it." Just then, Pooh and Piglet heard a sound in the distance.

"Hallooo!" Pooh turned to his friend. "I hope it isn't a fierce jagular. Because they 'Hallooo' and then drop on you." But it wasn't a jagular at all. It was only Tigger and Roo up in the tree. Pooh looked up. "How did you and Tigger get way up there?" "We bounced up!"

"Well, then, why don't you bounce down?" Pooh was very smart
for a bear of very little brain. And so, Roo bounced down.
But Tigger was still too frightened to jump that far. "Somebody, help!"
It wasn't long before word got to Christopher Robin that Tigger
was in trouble.

Everyone quickly came to his rescue, but no one knew what to do.
So I stepped in to help. "You see, Tigger? All your bouncing has
finally gotten you into trouble." "Who are you?"
"I'm the narrator." "Oh. Well, narrate me down from here.
If you do, I promise I'll never bounce again!"
So I turned the book sideways, and Tigger slid right down
the block of type to land safely on the ground.

Tigger was most relieved to be on solid ground again.
"I'm so happy, I feel like bouncing!"
Rabbit crossed his arms. "No, Tigger. You promised!"
"You mean, not even one teensy-weensy bounce?"
When Rabbit shook his head, Tigger turned
and walked away.

Roo tugged at Kanga's arm. "Mama, I like the old bouncy
Tigger best." And everyone agreed. So they gave Tigger his
bounce back and he leaped for joy. Even Rabbit had to admit it.
"Yes, I quite agree. A Tigger without his bounce is no
Tigger at all."